Meet the Mammoth!

School Specialty.
Publishing

Text Copyright © Evans Brothers Ltd. 2005. Illustration Copyright ©
Evans Brothers Ltd. 2005. First published by Evans Brothers Limited, 2A
Portman Mansions, Chiltern Street, London W1U 6NR, United
Kingdom. This edition published under license from Zero to Ten
Limited. All rights reserved. Printed in China. This edition published in
2005 by Gingham Dog Press, an imprint of School Specialty Publishing,
a member of the School Specialty Family.

Library of Congress-in-Publication Data is on file with the publisher.

Send all inquiries to:
School Specialty Publishing
8720 Orion Place
Columbus, OH 43240-2111

ISBN 0-7696-4187-3

1 2 3 4 5 6 7 8 9 10 EVN 10 09 08 07 06 05

Meet the Mammoth!

By Vivian French

Illustrated by Lisa Williams

GINGHAM DOG
PRESS

Columbus, Ohio

"Wah!" cried Cave Baby.
"Shhh!" said Cave Dad.

"Wah!" screamed
Cave Baby.

Thump!

8

"Mammoth!" shouted Cave Dad.

"Run!" screamed Cave Mom.

Thump! Thump!

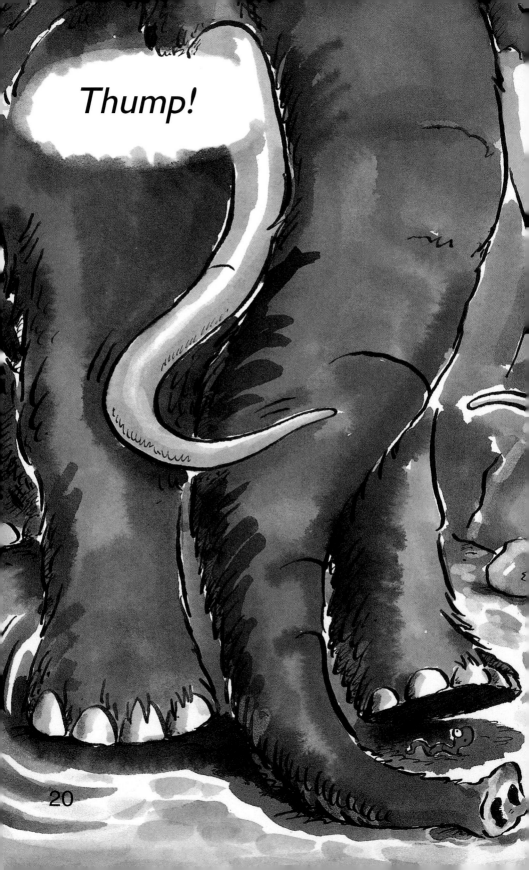

"Wah!" screamed Cave Baby.

23

Thump!

25

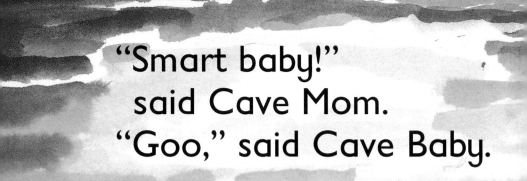

"Smart baby!"
said Cave Mom.
"Goo," said Cave Baby.

Words I Know

cried	screamed
baby	shouted
smart	where
cave	yelled

Think About It!

1. Why were Cave Mom, Cave Dad, and Cave Baby afraid?

2. What made the thumping noise?

3. What did Cave Dad tell Cave Mom and Cave Baby to do?

4. Why did the mammoth leave?

The Story and You

1. What sounds have you heard that made you afraid? What did you do about it?

2. Why would it be good to run away from something scary?

3. Talk about a time when you were brave.